ALBERT JOHNSON
AND THE
BUNS OF STEEL

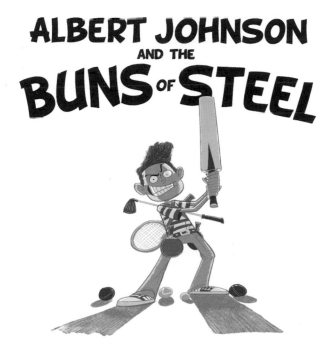

ALBERT JOHNSON
AND THE
BUNS OF STEEL

PHIL EARLE

Illustrated by
Steve May

Barrington Stoke

First published in 2021 in Great Britain by
Barrington Stoke Ltd
18 Walker Street, Edinburgh, EH3 7LP

www.barringtonstoke.co.uk

A CIP catalogue record for this book is available
from the British Library upon request

ISBN: 978-1-78112-907-4

Printed by Hussar Books, Poland

This book is in a super-readable format for young readers
beginning their independent reading journey.

For Albie (of course)
and also for Milton & Woody,
with love x

CONTENTS

CHAPTER 1

A FAMILY BUSINESS

Albert Johnson's family had always been bakers. Not just any bakers. Master Bakers. The most talented known to man.

There was his father, grandmother, great-grandmother, great-great-grandfather, great-great-great-grandfat—. You get the message.

There was nothing that Albert's dad couldn't shape out of dough.

A loaf like a swan? No problem.

A cake that looked like the Empire State Building? Easy.

A sliced white loaf the spitting image of Donald Trump?

... Well, you should probably see a doctor, but Albert's dad could bake you one anyway.

He was the best of the best and, boy, was he busy.

By 7 a.m. every day, the queue for the baker's shop stretched along the street. Customers dribbled like babies as the sweet smells invaded their nostrils.

But in order to make all that bread, Dad had to set his alarm for 2 a.m. to fire up the oven and knead his dough. Some nights he never went to bed at all.

This meant he had no time to spend with Albert, which made the boy feel, well, sad.

It also meant that Dad was pooped. So tired that he needed some help, which was where the problems began. And when I say problems, I mean PROBLEMS, as he (or rather Albert) nearly caused ... THE END OF THE WORLD!

CHAPTER 2
BIG SHOES TO FILL

"It's time, son," Dad yawned to Albert one evening.

"For what?"

"For you to follow in my footsteps, to start learning."

"About what?"

Dad frowned. "About baking, son. What else?"

Albert felt his stomach sink.

"When I was your age," Dad went on, "I became my dad's assistant. I was always in the kitchen, kneading, mixing, breaking eggs – learning everything so I could take over one day."

Albert was feeling sick. "But you're not old, Dad. You don't need me to take over yet. You've hardly got any grey hairs."

"That's as may be, but I'm too busy, son. So are you in?"

Dad knew what the answer should be. The same one that he and all his ancestors had given.

Which made what happened next very, very difficult ...

CHAPTER 3
SIMPLY THE BEST

"Would it be OK if I said no, Dad?"

"Eh? What?!" Dad couldn't believe what he was hearing. "I'd love to spend more time with you, and I like baking," said Albert, "but ... I prefer *eating* it to *doing* it."

Dad gasped in horror.

"I could never be as good as you – you're the best!" Albert hoped that last compliment would sweeten his dad up.

"But you're a Johnson, and baking's what Johnsons do!" Dad said.

"I know, Dad, but what ... well, what if I wanted to do something else?"

"What else is there?"

Albert frowned.

"Are you kidding me? Have you looked up from your muffin mix in the last five years? Have you been watching me at all?"

"Course I have!" Dad said, blushing.

"Then you'll know the thing that matters most to me is sport."

"Sport? What, like … football?"

"Yes, but not just that. There's cricket. And tennis. And golf."

"Golf????" Dad turned a funny colour.

"Yeah. Golf's cool. I don't mind what I play really, as long as there's a ball involved."

"You could make rock cakes for me. They're round," said Dad.

Albert shook his head.

"Donuts then!"

"It's not the same. I can't score a goal with a donut!"

Dad felt terrible. He couldn't believe what his son had told him, or that he hadn't noticed earlier. So he tried to hide his hurt feelings.

"Sport, eh?" Dad said. "How wonderful!" Then he walked away to have a little cry in private.

And, most importantly, to come up with a new plan ...

CHAPTER 4
THE SPORTING LIFE

While his dad was busy coming up with another plan, Albert got back to what he loved best – playing sport.

And Albert Johnson was not just good at sport, he was amazing.

When he dribbled a football, it was like it was glued to his boot. And his shot was like a cannon booming.

It was the same when he held a tennis racket, or a hockey stick, or a ping-pong paddle. He had power and style, but he also had a sporty brain. He knew when to hit the ball hard but also knew when spin was his greatest weapon.

Today he was on the golf course, club in hand and ball at his feet.

The flag, far away and tiny, flapped madly.

Albert swung the driver back slowly, speeding up as the club got nearer and nearer to the ball.

WHAZOOOOOOOOOOM!

The ball flew up into the sky. In fact Albert hit it so high that it vanished into the clouds.

He watched and waited, until at last it landed only metres from the flag.

"What a shot!" he shouted.

But the ball hadn't finished. It rolled until it fell into the hole with a lovely *plop*.

A hole in one! Most golfers waited a lifetime for the smallest chance of that happening, and Albert had done it before he was even at big school.

He was a wonder. The best of the best.

Which was just as well, as things were about to go horribly wrong ...

CHAPTER 5

SURPRISE!!!

While Albert was busy being sporty,
Dad was hard at work. He'd closed the
baker's shop for a week, but he wasn't
resting – lordy, no.

He'd been in his garage for days on
end, hammering and welding bits of

metal, sawing things apart and nailing other things together. He couldn't wait to show Albert what he'd been up to.

Albert watched as Dad rolled the most enormous object out from the workshop, hidden beneath a sheet.

"What have you got under there?" Albert asked.

"The answer to all our prayers, son. Something that will let me have a lie-in from time to time. I might even be able to play some sport with you."

Albert liked the sound of that. He had to admit that sometimes he felt lonely. He was fed up of playing tennis against the wall.

"Let me introduce you to the future. Say hello to the Doughmaster 5000."

And Dad whipped off the sheet, leaving Albert to gasp.

CHAPTER 6
WHOA ...

Albert had never seen anything like it, apart from in sci-fi movies.

There in front of him stood the biggest robot he had ever seen. It had eyes that could shoot laser beams, arms like tree trunks (only made of metal) and a belly that wasn't a belly at all but the most enormous oven ever.

"Wh-wh-what is that?"

Albert was scared. He could see it was only a machine, but there was something sinister about it, like it was giving him the evil eye.

"This is the Doughmaster 5000 – the answer to all our problems. I've programmed its computer with everything my dad taught me. It's going to do all the baking for us," Dad told him.

Albert wasn't sure. He still felt a bit scared.

"Will everything taste as good?"

"Yes! And while it's busy in the kitchen, I'll have more time to spend with you. Maybe you can even take me to the golf course?"

Albert smiled at this, but he still felt nervous.

Something smelt wrong, and it had nothing to do with his dad's baking.

CHAPTER 7
BUSY, BUSY, BUSY

Dad was right about the machine.
The Doughmaster 5000 was amazing.
Everything it made tasted like heaven.

But Dad was wrong about the
free time he'd get back. Because the
Doughmaster 5000's baking was so good,
the queue outside the shop got longer

and longer. Dad was busier than ever: he had to order more ingredients, serve more customers – even counting the money took longer than before.

And as a result, Albert was still playing tennis against the wall. Except for today. Today it was raining.

"You can sweep the kitchen floor for me instead," Dad said, and he pushed a broom into Albert's hands.

Albert grumbled and quickly grew bored.

"Stupid machine, stupid Dad, stupid iced buns."

The only way to cheer himself up was to grab a football and practise his skills. Within minutes he was much happier, pretending he was playing in the cup final.

"Here comes Albert Johnson," he dreamed. "He beats two defenders, sees the keeper off his line and shoots ..."

The problem was he forgot the game was in his head. He kicked the ball with a ferocious volley that slammed straight into the face of the Doughmaster 5000.

"Oh blimey, sorry," Albert said, then blushed. Why was he saying sorry to a robot? He had no idea, but at the same time he was sure that when the ball first whacked it, the machine's eyes glowed, just for a second, the angriest red.

"Don't be daft," Albert said to himself. "It's a machine, it can't get cross, you doofus."

So he put the thought to the back of his mind, collected his ball, turned off the lights and went to bed, to dream of sport. Of course.

CHAPTER 8

UH OH – HERE COMES TROUBLE

Midnight.

All was quiet. Except in the bakery's kitchen, where something was waking up for the first time.

It started with a crackle, then a short circuit that saw power surge through every part of its robot body and made its eyes not just glow but pulse.

For the last week, since Albert's dad had finished making the Doughmaster 5000, the robot had done what it was told.

It had baked and made thousands of people happy with its delicious buns.

But as it came alive for the first time, thanks to the ball that Albert had kicked against its head, the Doughmaster 5000 wasn't happy at all.

It was ANGRY.

The Doughmaster 5000 flexed its legs and arms, and felt its immense power, then ripped its plug out of the wall, turned its oven up to maximum and marched out of the bakery.

"The world loves my buns," it said in a deep voice, "but it has seen nothing yet!"

CHAPTER 9
WHAT? HOW? WHY?

Albert woke to chaos.

Screaming, crying and wailing. And all of it from Dad.

"What's up?" Albert asked.

"The Doughmaster 5000. Someone's stolen it!"

"Stolen it? How? It's a huge robot?!"

But Dad didn't have time to answer, as from outside came an explosion that knocked them off their feet.

"What in the name of chocolate muffins was that?" Dad squealed as they dashed outside.

There it stood – a baking monster brought to life and hell-bent on revenge. It looked bigger, stronger and ... angry!

The Doughmaster 5000 was firing rock cakes from its fists in every direction, knocking over bus stops and lamp posts, flipping cars over with a single bun.

"Doughmaster 5000!" yelled Dad. "You're ... alive???"

The robot turned to face them.

"Ah," it growled. "My master and his idiot boy."

"Bit rude." Albert frowned. His dad had obviously forgotten to include a polite chip in its database.

"I suppose it was," answered the Doughmaster 5000. "And actually, it's you, boy, that I have to thank for all this."

Albert gulped. "Do you?"

"Oh, yes. When you kicked that ball into my head last night, it did something strange to me. It scrambled my brain and set me free. I don't want to be a slave any more. I'll bake what I want, not what anyone tells me to."

And with that, the Doughmaster 5000 reached inside its oven-stomach, pulled out an armful of French sticks and threw them at Dad and Albert.

Albert dived for cover behind a car, but Dad was rooted to the spot, trapped in a cage made entirely from bread.

The Doughmaster 5000 had thrown the French sticks with such force that

they had stuck in the ground like

javelins, and now Dad was its prisoner.

"How did you do that?" Dad gasped. "How did you make the bread so tough?"

The monster just laughed. "These sticks are nothing – only a starter. Wait until you see what's for pudding!"

CHAPTER 10

SWEET REVENGE

The next thirty minutes were wonderful for the Doughmaster 5000 but not for everyone else.

It thundered through the streets, raining down pasties, bread, cakes and biscuits, all baked to a new recipe that made everything hard as steel and twice as dangerous.

The police arrived, but they were no match for the machine. It simply speed-baked a batch of rock cakes, then threw them with pinpoint accuracy, blocking their path.

Then the army turned up to help.

"Doughmaster 5000," came a voice from a tank. "This is the army. Put down your rock cakes and turn off your oven."

"Or what?" roared the robot.

"Or face your doom!" came the reply.

The Doughmaster 5000 screamed with laughter. "Oh, that's how it's going to be, is it?" it said, and threw a load of jam donuts at the tanks. The throws were so accurate that the donuts wedged inside the barrels of the tanks' long noses so they could no longer fire.

Seconds later, from inside each and every tank there were yells and squeals, then the soldiers inside began to escape from the hatches, covered in a red mess.

"Forget hand grenades," laughed the robot. "These are JAM GRENADES!"

Albert was terrified. The police and the army hadn't been able to help. Who knew when the Doughmaster 5000 would stop?

So without a thought for his own safety, Albert broke cover, dodged the cakes being hurled at him and sprinted back home. He needed to fetch his sports bag, and quickly.

CHAPTER 11
ALBERT HATCHES A PLAN

Hidden down an alley from the
Doughmaster 5000, Albert set down his
sports bag and got ready for a fight.

The bag weighed a ton, but if his
plan was going to work, he'd need every
single thing he'd stashed in there.

"Come on, you can do this," he said, kitting himself out with the only weapons he'd been able to lay his hands on.

He hooked his favourite table-tennis paddles through his belt loops and slipped a tennis racket, a golf club and a cricket bat over his shoulders, wearing them like an archer wears his bow and arrows.

He was almost ready.

Next, Albert pulled every ball he owned out of the bag: golf balls, tennis balls, hockey balls, it didn't matter.

"They aren't balls any more," he whispered to himself. "They're ammo."

He put the smaller ones in his pockets and then lined up all his footballs on the road.

Then Albert took six steps back and drew the hugest of breaths, knowing it could be his last.

It was now or never, do or die. He was Albert Johnson, and if he went down, he would go down fighting.

CHAPTER 12

WHAT A SHOT!!

The first football flew through the air. But Albert didn't have time to admire his shot; he had to go again and again and again.

He kicked ball after ball, then watched them spin and curl towards their target.

Every single one of them made contact with the Doughmaster 5000's head.

Boing! Boing! BOOING!

But the robot didn't flinch. In fact, he headed the balls straight back in Albert's direction, forcing him to dive behind a car.

Had Dad taught the machine about football too? Albert blooming well hoped not.

He grabbed his tennis racket. It was time for phase two.

"Let's do this," he yelled, sprinting from behind the car and firing every tennis ball that he had stuffed in his pockets.

He tried every stroke: forehands, backhands, serves, smashes. But it did no good. Every ball rebounded off the robot's body without leaving a mark.

"Pathetic!" the robot roared. "That's the second set to me. And it's my serve now!"

Without warning, the robot launched a HUGE lump of sloppy dough at Albert.

There was no time to run. All Albert could do was hold up his tennis racket and feel the dough hit it with a splat, before it oozed through to cover every inch of his face.

"Bleurgh!" he yelled as he fell to the ground.

This wasn't going well. The Doughmaster 5000 had an answer for everything, and Albert was quickly running out of both weapons and ammunition.

CHAPTER 13
WHAT NOW?

The air was filled with laughter.

"Too easy," the Doughmaster 5000 yelled. "Baker's sons are meant to be made from tougher stuff."

But Albert had not given up.

He pulled the cricket bat from his back. It felt good in his hands, like he could hit a hundred sixes with it, though all he had were three cricket balls tucked in his pockets.

But how would he launch an attack when the robot had both his eyes fixed so accurately on him?

Suddenly, from nowhere, out came Dad, with a tennis racket in his hand that looked about a hundred years old.

"You look like you need help, and I was pretty good at this before baking came along," he said.

Albert felt a rush of joy. He never knew his dad was sporty too. And, boy, did he need a partner.

So as Dad sprinted left and started firing balls at the robot, Albert dashed right and launched the most ferocious shot. This time it was a cricket ball, and it rocketed away and hit the monster's head. Albert saw the robot's head wobble.

"It's working, Dad!"

They both fought harder, a dream team in action.

Albert launched a second attack. It hit the target again! But now he only had one ball left and he had to make it count.

WHAAAAAAAACK!

THOIIIIINKKKKK!

The last ball hit the Doughmaster 5000's head, and again it wobbled. In fact, the robot knelt down and shook its head as if it was dizzy. Albert looked for another ball to launch, but there was nothing. His pockets were empty.

"Looking for this?" the Doughmaster 5000 shouted, holding Albert's cricket ball high in the air.

"Please can I have my ball back?" asked Albert.

No chance! Instead, the robot crushed the ball into dust with its right hand, before letting fly with a savage throw from its left.

"Try hitting this!" it yelled. But the throw was so fast, Albert couldn't even see it.

All he could do was close his eyes and swing his cricket bat.

The bat felt the mightiest impact and blew Albert off his feet.

I've done it, Albert thought to himself. *I must've whacked the ball right back at him. And if it hit him, then I must've won, I must've!!*

But when he opened his eyes, the Doughmaster 5000 was still stood there, oven blazing.

And Albert's bat had a huge hole in the middle of it.

"Oh no! How did that happen?" gasped Dad and Albert.

"My buns of steel, that's how," shouted the robot. "The hardest balls known to humankind. Nothing on earth can withstand their power."

The Doughmaster 5000 marched away to torment the rest of the world. There was nothing, and no one, that could stop him.

CHAPTER 14
THE FINAL SWING

Albert wasn't a quitter, but he and Dad were all out of ideas AND ammunition. All they could do was lie back and sob. But as Albert lay worn out on the ground, something dug into his back.

His golf club.

He sighed. What use was a club when he had nothing to hit? And anyway, there was no ball hard enough to put an end to the Doughmaster 5000's rampage.

But then the robot's final words about his buns of steel rang in Albert's ears so many times that it actually gave him an idea!

He jumped to his feet. "That's it!!!" he cried. "That's it!" and he began to search the rubble.

"What are you looking for?" said Dad.

But Albert couldn't hear him. The blood was pumping in his ears.

He stood, holding up a ball of cooked dough.

"Look!" he shouted. "A bun of steel!"

"A what?" said Dad.

"This is the hardest ball ever. Like the robot said, 'Nothing on earth can withstand its power'. NOTHING!"

Dad understood the plan and smiled. He'd never been prouder as Albert put the bun softly on the ground.

Albert breathed deeply.

This was it.

He had one bun.

One shot.

One chance to save the world.

"Oy! Doughmaster 5000!" he yelled.

The monster turned to face him.

"Eat this!" shouted Albert.

He swung the club and the bun fizzed into the distance. The robot laughed at the boy's latest attempt to destroy him. But then something strange happened.

The robot felt a breeze around his tummy, which never happened. His oven was always roaring. But as he looked down now, instead of a raging oven, there was just ... a hole. A huge, jagged hole.

"What did you do?" it sobbed at Albert. "How and what and why?"

But it never heard an answer. Its circuit board had caught fire and all its power drained quickly away.

First one knee, then another collapsed, until the whole machine packed up – leaving it a useless, smoking mess.

Albert collapsed to his knees too –
but not in pain, in sheer relief. Dad
hugged him, hard.

"What a shot!" Dad grinned. "I've
never seen anything like it. You blew its
oven clean out!"

"You should see what I can do on a
cricket pitch," Albert laughed.

"Can't wait," Dad cheered. "But first we should celebrate ... with a feast. You must be starving! I'll whip up the best buns you've ever tasted!"

But the thought of any more baking turned Albert more than a little green.

"I might settle for an apple. If that's OK."

And so an apple is just what they had. And, boy, did it taste good.

Our books are tested
for children and young people by
children and young people.

Thanks to everyone who consulted on
a manuscript for their time and effort in
helping us to make our books better
for our readers.